S0-AJO-916

CHRISTMAS COWBOY

JACKSON COUNTY LIBRARY SERVICES
MEDFORD OREGON 97501

WITHDRAWN
Damaged, Obsolete, or Surplus
Jackson County Library Services

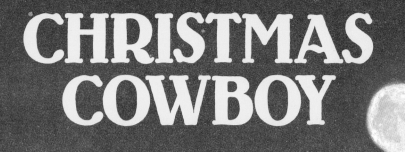

CHRISTMAS COWBOY

BY SARAH WILSON

ILLUSTRATED BY
PETER PALAGONIA

SIMON & SCHUSTER BOOKS FOR YOUNG READERS
Published by Simon & Schuster
New York   London   Toronto   Sydney   Tokyo   Singapore

SIMON & SCHUSTER BOOKS FOR YOUNG READERS
Simon & Schuster Building, Rockefeller Center
1230 Avenue of the Americas, New York, New York 10020.
Text copyright © 1993 by Sarah Wilson.
Illustrations copyright © 1993 by Peter Palagonia.
All rights reserved including the right of reproduction
in whole or in part in any form.
SIMON & SCHUSTER BOOKS FOR YOUNG READERS
is a trademark of Simon & Schuster.
Manufactured in the United States of America

10 9 8 7 6 5 4 3 2 1

Library of Congress Cataloging-in-Publication Data
Wilson, Sarah. Christmas cowboy / by Sarah Wilson;
illustrated by Peter Palagonia. Summary: The joy of Christmas
is restored to a harsh, forgotten valley by a mysterious cowboy
who comes to stay awhile. [1. Christmas—Fiction.
2. Cowboys—Fiction.] I. Palagonia, Peter, ill. II. Title.
PZ7.W6986Ch 1992 [E]—dc20 CIP 91-712
ISBN 0-671-74780-0

For Father John C. Henrick,
who carries the spirit of Christmas within him
SW

For my family
PP

Once not so very long ago, an old cowboy wandered into a rough-board town in a dry, forgotten valley. It was a place where people worked long and hard for very little and the weather was always too hot or too cold for them. But worst of all, hardly anybody ever laughed there, not even the children!

The cowboy had a sunburned face and sky-blue eyes. His clothes were patched and tattered, and he was on foot, without the shadow of a horse in sight.

"You must have walked a long way!" one of the men said.

The cowboy just smiled. He didn't say a word about where he'd come from, only that he'd received a message he was needed there.

Who could have sent the cowboy a message?

People shook their heads. But in the distance, in the rafters of an ancient barn, an old barn owl and a family of field mice jumped up and down with excitement.

"No Christmas here and no miracles for thirty years come last Tuesday" was the message they'd sent with a hawk, who had flown with it to an eagle, who had carried it to a wild goose, who had taken it to a snowbird, who had disappeared with it

into the coldest, quietest part of the northern skies, where earth lights dance among the stars. And now, here was a cowboy.

The cowboy wasn't who the owl and the field mice had expected, but they were happy to see him.

The people of the town were drop-mouth astonished. But they knew what it was like to be cast adrift in hard country and poor as they were, they set about feeding the cowboy and finding him a place to sleep.

This turned out to be a storage shed for what had once been a raggle-taggle circus—and the same place where the old barn owl and the field mice made their home.

"Now, what's going on here?" the cowboy asked the owl and the mice. (He was one of those special, rare people who can talk with animals.)

The old owl sighed. "The families in this valley have forgotten miracles," he said.

"But *we* remember!" a young field mouse told the cowboy, who stroked her ears as gently as if they were made of silk.

"Let's see what we can do then," said the cowboy, going out with them to see the valley.

There men at their jobs worked without a wink or a whistle or even a passing wonder, and women in their houses saw only chores piled upon chores upon chores. And children in the school yard sat waiting for recess to end without a happy face among them!

With December fast approaching, the old cowboy stopped each child and asked the same question over and over: "When do you write your letters to Santa Claus?"

They all shook their heads. Nobody wrote letters to Santa Claus.

"Who *is* Santa Claus?" a small boy wanted to know.

So the old cowboy sat down and tried to explain not only Santa Claus but Christmas—the time of year to remember love and miracles and the celebration of being together.

"There isn't time for miracles here!" said a weary father.

"Then I'll have to stay for a while," said the old cowboy,
and that same night he and the owl and the field mice
began poking around the storage barn to see what they
could find. They uncovered bits and pieces of old
carrousel animals that were now broken and aban-
doned, wagon wheels and dusty paint cans, rusted
tools and empty gear boxes, and one jingle bell
left over from a forgotten Christmas.

The old cowboy beamed. "Well, *somebody*
remembered!" he said, putting the bell in
his boot. "This may come in handy later!"

For the next few days, the cowboy chopped wood and hammered shingles and helped with the laundry, humming as he worked and sometimes stopping to do a hop and a dance on a worn wooden floor. And all this time he kept asking the children, "What would you want if you could have anything that stirs in your heart?"

The children weren't used to being asked about what they wanted, and certainly not about what stirred in their hearts (whatever that meant), so they took a long time to answer.

"Horses," they said finally, one by one by one.

"Done!" said the cowboy at each answer, sounding as if each child's wish had somehow been granted and making a note of it in a ragged little book he kept in his back pocket.

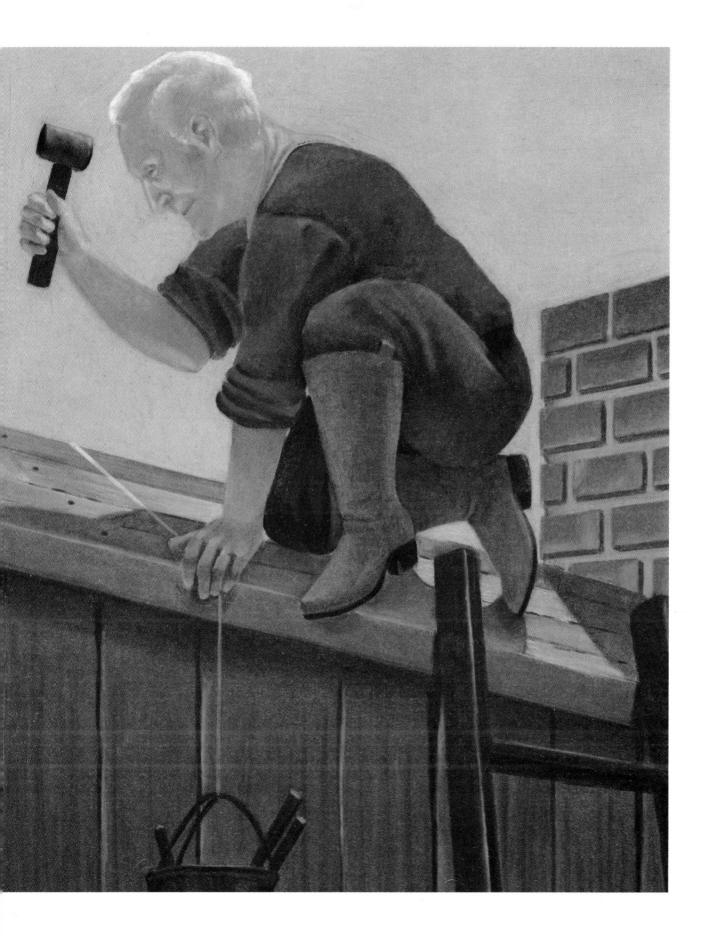

He went on with his work for a day or two more, then suddenly announced that he had to be going. "Christmas will be coming soon," he told the people in the valley, "and others are waiting for me."

No one could imagine who was waiting for an old cowboy living in the middle of nowhere, but they went about helping him finish the things he wanted to do before he left. They gathered up old tumbleweeds with him and set them around their houses, then watched in amazement as he showed them how to decorate the tall bushes with scraps and ribbons and yarn ends, and corn husk toys and wood shavings, and then from somewhere, candle cups and tiny candles.

"On the night before Christmas, light the candles," the old cowboy told them. "Gather your families together and wait...."

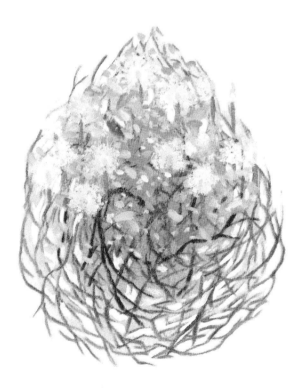

"For what?" the people wanted to know.
"For your presents," said the cowboy before he
bundled himself in blankets and walked out of
the town just as he had come in, leaving by the

same road and in a falling snow. This time,
though, there was a barn owl on one shoulder
and a family of field mice held warm in his
pockets and under his cap.

That seemed to be the end of things but, of course, it wasn't, for in the long winter darkness that fell over the valley, people felt something new. The excitement kept building until Christmas Eve night, when families gathered in the snow around their houses and the lights on the tumbleweed trees shone like stars. They didn't know that the cowboy was back again and in the old barn where he had slept.

Smiling, the cowboy touched the small jingle bell from his boot to a handful of bells from his pocket, beginning a spark that lit up the barn as bright as a sunrise and set lost things to stirring in all of its far corners.

As the light grew and grew and the old owl and the field mice cheered, wooden objects became whole again and new, turning into carrousel horses and other animals with coats of fresh paint and bells and saddles!

They lifted from the floor, nudging and neighing, until the
cowboy flung open the barn doors and set them free
into the night. There they went flying toward the tumbleweed trees in the town, each one to a child.

Those who watched at the edge of the valley saw
it all: the trees, the carrousel animals, and something
else—the old cowboy and the owl and the mice lift-
ing up over the hills in a big red wagon, waving as
they flew over the sounds of laughter from the
children below.

It made an old cowboy—who is now settled back into the coldest, quietest part of the northern skies, where earth lights dance among the stars—very, very content.